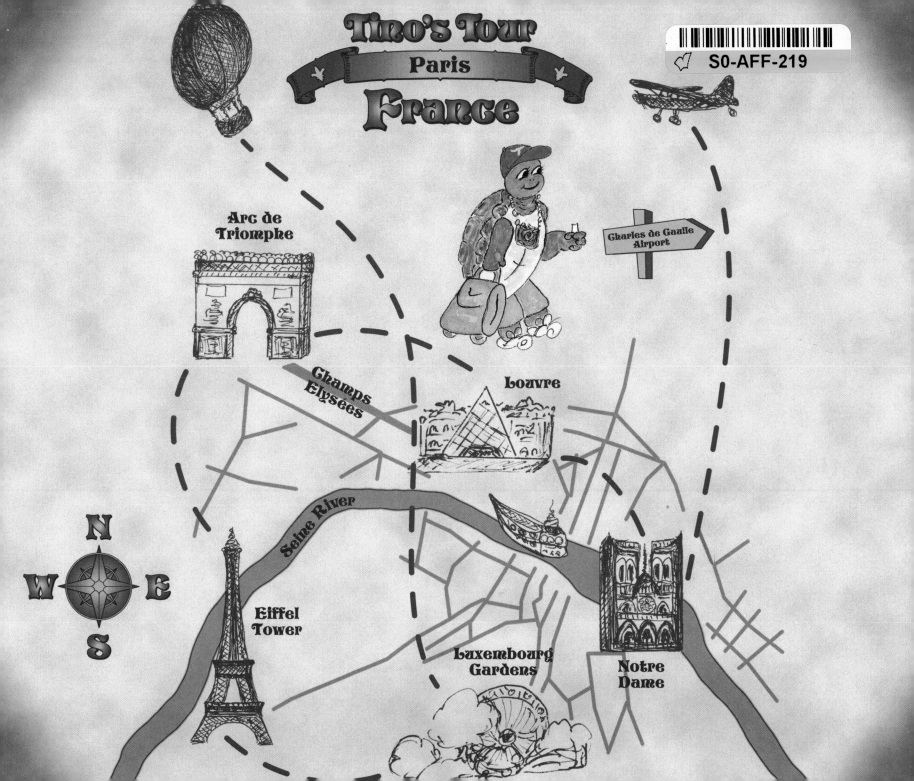

This Book Belongs To:

_____

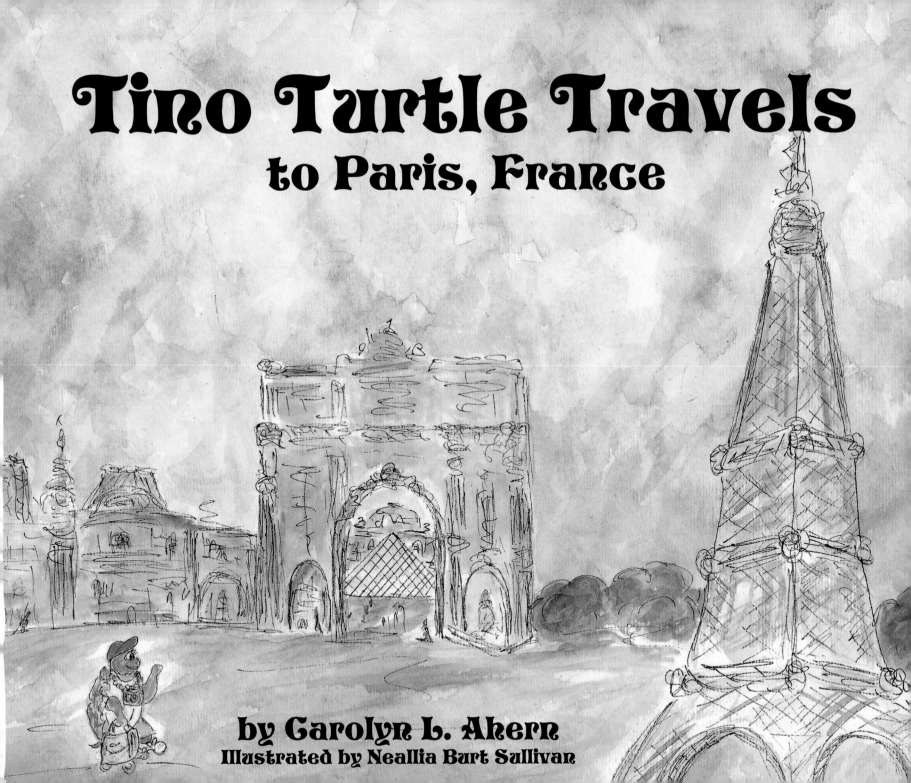

Tino Turtle Travels
to Paris, France

by Carolyn L. Ahern

Illustrated by Neallia Burt Sullivan

To my husband, Don F. Ahern
To the sweet spirit of Dayna Lynn Ahern
———————— & ————————
To my parents, Frank and Sue Bella
Thank you for believing in Tino

Tino Turtle Travels, LLC
8550 West Charleston Boulevard, Suite 102-398
Las Vegas, Nevada 89117
Copyright © 2006 by Carolyn L. Ahern

info@TinoTurtleTravels.com
www.TinoTurtleTravels.com

The artwork was executed in watercolor, watercolor pencils,
graphite and colored inks on Strathmore cold press paper.
The text was set in 16-point New Century Schoolbook,
24-point Barmeno, and 24-point Storybook.

Written and created by Carolyn L. Ahern.

Printed in the USA.

Library of Congress Control Number: 2007924999

ISBN-13: 978-0-9793158-1-7

ISBN-10: 0-9793158-1-6

TINO TURTLE TRAVELS and the TINO logo
are trademarks of Tino Turtle Travels, LLC.

Once upon a time, there was a desert tortoise named Tino. Tino was a happy turtle in his desert habitat, but he had one wish...he dreamed of traveling to see the world.

One night, when in his burrow for his winter sleep, he asked his Fairy God Turtle to make his wish come true.

"Please Fairy God Turtle...
let me travel."

When Tino closed his eyes, his Fairy God Turtle waved her magic wand and granted Tino's wish.

Whoosh! Suddenly, Tino is on his way to Paris, France...far, far away from his desert burrow.

Tino spends the long flight across the Atlantic Ocean sleeping, watching movies and reading. Hoping to learn more about the city he is visiting, he reads the Paris Daily Newspaper.

An ad in the paper catches his attention:

"FRIEND WANTED AT PARIS ORPHANAGE. ASK FOR MONIQUE."

"Humm," Tino ponders, "I could use a friend to show me around Paris."

After Tino arrives at *Charles de Gaulle* airport in Paris, he hurries to find a ride to the orphanage. He hears a voice call out in a French accent:

"HOT AIR BALLOON RIDES!"

"Wow!" says Tino, "That looks like fun! I think I'll give it a try."

"Ahhh, *Bonjour Monsieur,* my name is Tino Turtle and I'm from America. I'd like to go for a balloon ride and see your city, *s'il vous plaît.*"

The balloon pilot introduces himself. "*Je m'appelle* Pierre-Louis. I am the pilot of the biggest and fastest balloon in all of Paris. Hop in and I'll show you the finest our city has to offer!"

Swoosh! The balloon's burners roar...lifting them up into the sky. Pierre-Louis shouts, "Up, up and away!"

"What a blast!" Tino exclaims. "Excuse me *Monsieur,* would you mind if we drop in at the city orphanage? There is someone there I want to meet."

"Of course," Pierre-Louis answers. "Hang on tight to the ropes and watch how fast this balloon can go!"

Tino squeals with delight..."Whee! Whee! Faster, faster!"

Kerplunk! The balloon lands
right in front of the orphanage.

A nice lady greets Tino at the door.

"*Bonjour Madame.* My name is Tino Turtle. I'm from America. Are you the orphanage mother? I am sorry, my French is not very good."

"*Bonjour* Tino. My name is *Madame* Marie-Élise. I am the director. How may I help you?"

"Ahhh, well, I am looking for *Mademoiselle* Monique. I saw her name in the newspaper. Does she live here?"

Just then, a little girl's face appears
peeking out from behind the lady.

"Oh Monique, don't be shy," says *Madame*
Marie-Élise, "There is no need to hide.
Come around and meet the new friend
you asked for…his name is Tino."

Monique is very surprised to see that a turtle has come to visit and greets Tino with a hesitant smile. She can see that her special visitor is very nice and is happy that her ad in the newspaper has been answered.

"There is a balloon waiting for us, Monique. Will you show me around your city, please?"

Monique's face brightens with excitement.

"*S'il vous plaît, Madame,* may I go?"

"Monique, you may go, but you must return to the orphanage before bedtime."

"Oh, I will! *Merci beaucoup, Madame.*"

"Come on Monique, let's jump in the balloon!"

Pierre-Louis greets Monique and says, *"Bonjour Mademoiselle. Prepare for take off!"*

They both hold on to the balloon ropes and cheer, "Yippee, Yippee!"

Tino is so excited that he starts to dance around in the balloon basket…twirling and whirling, until he gets dizzy!

Monique starts to giggle as she watches Tino acting silly. Then they both burst out laughing.

"What's that?" Tino asks.

Monique answers, "It must be a bird from the *Luxembourg* Palace & Gardens below."

They stare in awe as an amazing bird flies by...its wings a rainbow of colors.

"The *Luxembourg* Palace & Gardens is home to the French Senate. Also, nearby is a playground with fun rides, *marionnettes* shows and lots of ice cream! Let's start our city tour there."

Pierre-Louis nods in agreement and lands the balloon softly in the park grass. The beautiful palace glistens in the sunlight.

Tino and Monique head for the Ferris wheel ride.

After the Ferris wheel stops, they are off to the next ride. "Let's hurry, Monique! I want to ride those beautiful painted horses on the merry-go-round."

"Ok Tino, you lead the way!"

They each pick their favorite horse to ride, and round and round they go. Tino teaches Monique to shout "Yee haw!" just like the cowboys back in his desert home.

After the ride ends, Tino exclaims, "This park is a blast, but I'm ready for some food to calm my hungry tummy. Do you think you can find something special for me to eat, Monique?"

"Let me think," Monique replies, "I know! I'll take you for *escargots!*"

"What is that?" Tino asks with a puzzled look on his face.

"It means *snails*…a real French delicacy!" Monique answers, "They are *délicieux!*… or as you would say, delicious!" she adds with a big grin. "Come with me!"

Before Monique could say *Bon appétit,*
Tino has already gobbled up the snails.

"Wow, these *escargots* are *délicieux!*" he
says with a satisfied smile.

"Let's get some *crème glacée* for dessert."
says Monique.

"What's that?" Tino questions.

"It's ice cream!"

Then, Monique has an idea…"Tino, would
you like to see a *marionnettes* show next?"

"Well, okay," he says, "but what kind of
show is that?"

CRÊPES

GLACIER

Patiss

"It's a puppet show. Look over there! It's about to start!"

"That sounds great, Monique. Let's go!"

After enjoying the wonderful puppet show, they get back in the balloon to continue their adventure.

"Can you guess what one of Paris' most famous monuments is?" asks Pierre-Louis.

"It's *la Tour Eiffel!*" blurts out Monique, "It is named after the designer, *Gustave Eiffel.*"

"Oh, *s'il vous plaît Monsieur,* take us there," begs Tino.

A few moments later, through the billowing clouds, the Eiffel Tower appears. Pierre-Louis carefully positions his balloon near the top of the tower.

"Wow! That is amazing! I've never seen anything that tall!" Tino exclaims.

"This tower was built in 1889 to celebrate the 100th birthday of the French Revolution," explains Pierre-Louis. "It's made of steel and stands 986 feet tall. To climb it, you would have to climb 1652 stairs to reach the top!"

"WOW!" Tino responds, "I don't think I'll try climbing it today!"

Swoosh! The balloon is off to a new destination.

Soon, they land on a look-out deck.

"Where are we?" Tino asks.

"We are now on the *Arc de Triomphe.*" Pierre-Louis replies, "It is a monument remembering the battle victories of our famous French Emperor, *Napoléon Bonaparte,* of long ago."

Tino is so curious he can't stop asking questions.

"What's that wide, wide street just ahead of us?"

"It's *les Champs-Elysées.*" Pierre-Louis explains, "It's known as one of the most beautiful avenues in the world!"

"Look over there, Tino! It's my favorite museum...*le Louvre!* It has one of the world's greatest collections of art!" Monique explains with enthusiasm.

Pierre-Louis adds, "It has many paintings by famous artists, such as *Claude Monet* and *Pierre-Auguste Renoir.*"

"Hold on friends, we're headed down!" shouts Pierre-Louis.

The balloon makes a swift landing next to the towering pyramid of the *Louvre*.

"Oh, can we go in?" begs Tino.

"Yes, but don't stay too long!" Pierre-Louis urges.

"Okay, *Monsieur* Pierre-Louis, we'll see you before dark," Monique replies.

They are anxious to get up close to the modern addition of the *Louvre,* known as *la pyramide.* Shimmering above them, the glass panels of the pyramid appear grand and tall.

Tino says, "I feel like a little ant next to this pyramid and scared that I'm going to fall through it."

"Not to worry, Tino. The glass is thick and strong. You won't fall," Monique reassures. "Come on, Tino. Let's go see the galleries."

Tino sees the entrance to the gallery and worries that his turtle legs are too slow for the distance. He notices some children in strollers and thinks to himself, "I wish I could be pushed in a stroller..." But Tino is too embarrassed to ask.

Suddenly, Monique screams, "*Attention!* Look out, everyone! There's a black widow spider crawling on the glass window!"

"Oh no!" Tino shouts, "It just swooped down onto that baby's stroller."

Tino s-t-r-e-t-c-h-e-s his neck and grabs the spider with his jaws! He tosses it onto a nearby tree, away from all the people.

"Great job, Tino! You protected *le bébé* and all of us!" Monique exclaims. "Let me reward you by giving you a ride in a stroller. You sure deserve it!"

She gets a stroller, and Tino crawls up into it with a big smile and a look of relief on his face.

They stroll through the art galleries and view paintings, amazing sculptures and ancient artifacts.

They've had an incredible journey exploring the museum, but it's time to get back to the balloon. Searching for an exit, they head for a sign that reads *SORTIE*.

Just outside the door awaits Pierre-Louis with his balloon.

Pierre-Louis says, "We better keep moving, so we can get you back before bedtime, Monique." He fires up the balloon's burners and lifts up high into the sky with a loud roar.

"I now have the pleasure of taking you to *Notre Dame*. It is one of my favorite *cathédrales*," says Pierre-Louis.

Tino stares in awe at *Notre Dame* below them.

Suddenly, they hear thunderous sounds in the sky!

"POP! POP! BOOM! BOOM! BOOM!"

Afraid of the strange sounds, Tino quickly hides his head inside his shell.

"Oh Tino, don't be frightened. Come on out. It's just the city celebrating with fireworks," explains Monique.

"Look how the fireworks light up *Notre Dame,*" says Pierre-Louis.

He adds, "This Gothic style *cathédrale* took about 200 years to build. And Tino, notice the rose windows…they are like shiny gems sure to dazzle your eyes!"

"You're right, *Monsieur* Pierre-Louis. It is an amazing church!" says Monique.

Stunned, Tino nods his head in agreement.

On their way back to the orphanage, the moon and stars light up the sky. They follow the reflection of the river that flows below them.

Winding through the night sky, as if they are floating through a maze, Monique says, "Tino, down below is *la Seine*. This river runs through the very heart of our city. Remember it, and always keep me in your heart, too…okay?"

"Okay Monique, I will."

They land at the orphanage just in time for Monique's bedtime. *Madame Marie-Élise* is waiting.

Monique hugs her new little friend goodbye and says, "*Au revoir*, Tino. Dont' forget to write me!"

"I won't," Tino says, "*Au revoir*, Monique."

Tino realizes that it is getting late for him as well. Spring would soon arrive, he would wake from hibernation and his dream would end.

"Please take me to the airport," he asks Pierre-Louis, "I must return to America."

Pierre-Louis replies, "Very well, to *l'aéroport* we must go!"

PARIS

Charles de Gaulle
Paris, France

At the airport, Tino boards the plane. He turns to wave one last goodbye to Pierre-Louis and the city that has captured his heart.

"The balloon tour has been a great adventure! *Au revoir et merci!*"

Waving back to Tino, Pierre-Louis says, *"Bon voyage, Tino!"*

Tino's Fairy God Turtle waves her magic wand, and…

Whoosh! Suddenly, Tino is back home in his desert burrow. His eyes open to the warmth of a spring breeze, the sound of birds singing and the smell of cactus blossoms.

Tino joyfully says out loud, "My dream of traveling the world has come true. Thank you Fairy God Turtle…'til next time we travel…Thank you."

THE END

Tino Turtle Travels to Paris, France – Glossary

French	Pronunciation	Meaning
Arc de Triomphe	*ahrk de tree-onf*	Largest triumphal arch in the world
Attention!	*atahs-yoh*	Look out!
Au revoir!	*ohr-vwar*	Goodbye!
Au revoir et merci!	*ohr-vwar ay mehr-see*	Goodbye and thank you!
Bon appétit!	*bun-apay-tee*	Enjoy your meal!
Bonjour Madame!	*boh-zhoor ma-dahm*	Hello Madam!
Bonjour Mademoiselle!	*boh-zhoor mad-mwa-zehl*	Hello Miss!
Bonjour Monsieur!	*boh-zhoor me-sy-uh*	Hello Mister!
Bon voyage!	*boh vwa-ya-zh*	Have a nice trip!
Cathédrale	*Ka-tay-dral*	Cathedral; Large church
Charles de Gaulle	*shahrl de gohl*	President of the French Fifth Republic 1958-69
Claude Monet	*kloed moh-nay*	French impressionist painter 1840 - 1926
Crème glacée	*krehm gla-say*	Ice Cream
Délicieux!	*day-lee-sy-uh*	Delicious!
Escargots	*ehs-kar-go*	Snails
Gustave Eiffel	*goos-taf eye-fuhl*	French engineer who designed the Eiffel Tower 1832 – 1923
Je m'appelle…	*zhem-ap-ehl*	My name is…
L'aéroport	*l-a-ay-rup-or*	Airport
La pyramide	*la pee-ra-meed*	Largest metal and glass pyramid (Louvre pyramid)
La Seine	*la sen*	Seine River – long river flowing through the heart of Paris
La Tour Eiffel	*la toor eye-fuhl*	Eiffel Tower
Les Champs-Elysées	*lay shahn zay-lee-zay*	Elysian Fields – considered most famous avenue in the world
Le bébé	*le bay-bay*	Baby
Le Louvre	*le loo-vruh*	Largest, oldest, most famous art museum in Paris
Luxembourg	*lewx-ah-boor*	Luxembourg (Palace & Gardens) – Home to the French Senate
Madame	*ma-dahm*	Madam
Marionnettes	*mar-yo-net*	Marionettes; Puppets
Merci beaucoup!	*mehr-see bo-koo*	Thank you very much!
Napoléon Bonaparte	*nuh-poe-layoh boh-nuh-pahrt*	French general and emperor 1769 – 1821
Notre Dame	*noh-truh dahm*	Our Lady – Gothic style cathedral
Pierre-Auguste Renoir	*pyer oe-goost ren-wahr*	French impressionist painter 1841 – 1919
S'il vous plaît!	*seel-voo-pleh*	Please!
SORTIE	*sor-tee*	EXIT

Tino Turtle Travels
to Paris, France

Words and Music by Sue Bella